BLUEBLOOD

Malorie Blackman

WITH ILLUSTRATIONS BY

Laura Barrett

VINTAGE

Chapter One - Nia

ONCE UPON A TIME – maybe last year, maybe even last month – there was a woman called Nia. Now I guarantee you've seldom, if ever, met anyone like her before. Who was she? She was a woman who never wrote on lined paper, that's who. Why should she allow herself to be confined by the lines on a page? That was her life philosophy. Nothing was going to pin her down or hold her back or hem her in. How old was she? The question was always met with the same reply. 'Ha! Numbers are for maths teachers.'

Her height? Her weight?

Same answer!

Her star sign? 'Please! As if I'd believe in that nonsense!' Her words, not mine.

Let's put it this way – she knew her worth. And like all women who have had to work to know their place and purpose in the world, she was a woman on a mission.

And what was that mission?

Why, to get married of course!

Marcus was the perfect candidate. He was smart. I mean, he wanted to marry her, didn't he? In fact, he was desperate to have Nia as his wife. When they first got engaged, Nia's younger brothers, Jakob and Desmond, gave her all kinds of grief – though for different reasons.

'Nia, not again! He's double your age for a start!' said Jakob.

'He's fifteen years older, not double. And what does that have to do with anything?' Nia said.

'Fifteen years older! Eww! That's just nasty. That's practically Jurassic, ' said Desmond, the younger brother. 'And that beard of his – it's so thick and crusty-looking, you'll need a hedge trimmer and at least an hour to find his lips.'

'Desmond, behave! Besides, his beard is his best feature. And if you must know, he offered to shave it off completely, but I wouldn't let him.'

'He's got shifty eyes, Nia. "All the better to constantly watch you with, my dear,"' warned Jakob.

'Maybe that's why I'm marrying him.'

Jakob and Nia exchanged a knowing look. Watching both of them with a frown, Desmond asked, 'What does that mean?'

'It means Marcus loves me so much, he wants me with him twenty-four/seven,' Nia replied lightly. 'Isn't that romantic?'

'No, that's just messed up,' Desmond argued.

Nia smiled and stroked her brother's cheek. 'Des, please don't ever change.'

'Sis, you can do better,' Desmond persisted.

'Marcus is exactly what I've been looking for.'

'That's what you said about all the others before they disappeared on you,' Desmond pointed out. 'What makes you think this one will be any different?'

'He's the son of a High Court judge –'

'That's his dad's job –'

'His mum's job, actually,' Nia corrected.

4

'Who cares! What's Marcus's job? How does he make his money?'

'Import–export.'

'What does that even mean?' asked Desmond.

'Nia, please, I'm begging you. Don't do this,' said Jakob. 'He's not worth it – and you can do so much better. Why won't you believe you deserve to be happy? Truly happy.'

Jakob's question made Nia inwardly wince. She glared at her brothers. They were really beginning to dance on her nerves.

'Both of you know how I feel about people telling me what to do. I'm marrying Marcus and that's all there is to it.'

When Nia's brothers opened their mouths to argue some more, Nia raised a hand.

'ENOUGH. I hear one more disparaging remark about my fiancé and neither of you will be invited to our wedding.'

And with that, the comments ceased.

In spite of her family – or maybe because of them – Marcus and Nia made their wedding plans sooner rather than later. If Nia had had her way, she and Marcus would've eloped and had done

with it, but Marcus argued that the fastest way to get both of their families to accept their marriage was to make them a part of the wedding. So Nia went along with his wishes – against her better judgement.

Also against her better judgement, Nia realised in the weeks before her wedding just how much she liked her fiancé. Oh she loved him – that part happened naturally. But to her surprise, she discovered just how much she liked him; his bad jokes, the way he gave her his coat when she was chilly, the way he knew how to hold a decent conversation, the way he held her hand just because. She liked being with him. Loving him was comfortable. Liking him made her . . . uneasy. All she could do was hope against hope that her brothers – and the rumours – were wrong about Marcus and that he wouldn't turn out to be like all the others.

Chapter Two ~ Marcus

MARCUS HAD NEVER met anyone like Nia before. Unstintingly kind, she always asked about his health and his day and was genuinely interested in his replies in a way he'd rarely experienced before. Every time he looked into her dark brown eyes, he could feel himself falling just a little bit more in love with her. What's more, she even liked his beard, though she insisted he keep it neat and trim. Most of his previous partners had constantly nagged at him to shave it off.

'Your beard is so black, in certain lights it looks almost midnight blue. I love you – you and your midnight beard!' she teased.

At first Marcus loved that Nia was so open and friendly, but after a while, when he realised she was that way with everyone, her amiability began to grate. Did she have to be quite so sociable? She treated everyone the same – friend and stranger alike – but he was her fiancé and soon to be her husband. He should take priority over everyone else. Never mind. Once they were married, Marcus was sure he would be the focus of Nia's attention. Her brothers irritated him most of all – always trying to poke their unwanted noses into his business.

And as for the malicious gossip about his fiancée? Marcus didn't even listen to it. So what if she'd been married before and her husband had run off and left her? She'd divorced him afterwards so that chapter of her life was closed. And she ran her own successful jewellery-making business so why would she be only after his money, as some of his friends had suggested? Her jewellery designs were

sought after by celebrities around the world and sold in exclusive boutiques for staggering sums.

Marcus didn't appreciate just how successful Nia really was until the first time he visited her three-storey, five-bedroom home. As Nia showed him around, he grew more and more flustered, though he did his best to hide it. He had money in the bank but he strongly suspected that Nia had far more.

'This house has been in my family for generations,' Nia answered his unasked question. 'As the oldest, it was left to me when my father died.'

Each bedroom had its own bathroom, plus she had a three-car garage and her vast back garden was filled with mature fruit trees, exotic flower borders, a summer house and a lawn so immaculate it looked like it had been sprayed on the ground rather than growing out of it. Nia's house even had its own lift. One of the old-fashioned kind with a steel, lattice-work manual door that had to click and lock into place before the lift would move. The back wall of the lift was a mirror and on the front panel were six buttons: 3, 2, 1, G, a blank red button which it was impossible to press and a yellow Help button, with assistance guaranteed to arrive within the hour – day or night. Through Nia's hard work she'd created her dream home and career – and it made Marcus love her even more.

'As my home is more than big enough for both of us, why don't you sell your flat and move in here?' said Nia.

She only had one condition.

'The attic space will be all yours. The whole floor. You can turn it into a study, a den, a workshop or whatever you want to call it. I won't go into your room.' Nia favoured Marcus with a hard stare. 'But by the same token, you don't get to enter my study in the basement. Ever.'

Marcus frowned. 'Your study? Why haven't you shown that to me yet?'

Nia sighed. 'Marcus, what did I just say? My study is my private space. You don't get to enter it. If our relationship is going to work then I need you to respect my wishes.'

'Of course,' Marcus replied. 'No problem. You'll stay out of the attic and I'll stay out of the basement.'

'I want your word,' Nia insisted.

'I promise to stay out of your study,' said Marcus, though he couldn't help thinking, What's the big deal? I have seen a desk and a chair before.

But he kept that to himself. If Nia required a promise to be comfortable with him in her own home, then so be it. Marcus knew in his heart he'd found the woman with whom he wanted to spend the rest of his life. And with a few well-chosen lies and a little luck, hopefully she'd never discover his secret.

Chapter Three ~ Nia

URING THEIR FIRST FEW WEEKS of marriage, Nia began to wonder if perhaps the reports about Marcus were just so much vicious gossip. Maybe the so-called facts she'd been given regarding his past were mere unproven speculations. However, slowly but surely Marcus's true colours began to shine through. With every interrogation or accusation, the fog of pretence surrounding him lifted just a little bit more to reveal what lay beneath. Each morning during breakfast Marcus asked, 'What will you be doing today?'

'Working for a few hours in the basement,' Nia replied.

'Doing what – exactly?'

'Designing jewellery. Probably making a test piece or two.'

'May I see?' said Marcus.

'I'll show you a couple of designs over dinner tonight.'

'Well, I hope they're less gaudy than most of your past efforts,' said Marcus with disdain.

Nia shrugged. 'You may not like them but you're not exactly my target customer.'

'Why can't I go down to the basement and see your designs now?'

'Marcus, you know you're not supposed to ask that.'

'You spend practically every morning and most afternoons down there. I'm curious, that's all.'

'Don't forget what curiosity did to the cat,' Nia reminded him, her shaped eyebrows arched in warning.

'What harm would it do?'

Nia sighed. 'It's the principle of the thing. I'm more than happy to share my home with you but I need a space and a place that's mine and mine alone. We agreed to this – remember?'

This bone of contention appeared each day with their morning coffee and usually left by the time the coffee was drunk so Nia tried to let it go. But Marcus was starting to behave in ways he hadn't before. Every time she tried to set foot out of the house, Nia was met with a list of questions:

Where are you going?

Who are you going to see?

When will you be back?

Why d'you need to go out?

Why can't I come with you?

At first Nia tried to put it down to the fact that they were newly-weds. After all, wasn't it only natural that Marcus would want the two of them to spend as much time together as possible?

'I do have other friends, Marcus. I love you but that doesn't mean we're joined at the hip and have to do absolutely everything together,' Nia said gently.

But Marcus couldn't hear her, or perhaps he just stopped listening. The questioning grew steadily worse, as if Marcus resented Nia spending even one minute away from him. When she wouldn't let him accompany her to nights out with her friends, Marcus's questions took on a nastier tone.

'Why can't I come with you? What're you hiding?'

'Marcus, enough! Stop this,' Nia pleaded.

But he wouldn't or couldn't stop. After five months of marriage, Nia had no choice but to acknowledge that all the rumours and speculation about Marcus had been true. Their latest blazing row happened when an opportunity for a trip abroad to investigate a new source of precious gems came up and Nia wouldn't turn it down.

'If you really cared about our marriage, you wouldn't go,' said Marcus.

Disappointed, Nia shook her head. 'Marcus, this is my job. I'll only be gone a week. Ten days at most. You have all the keys and codes for the house so there shouldn't be a problem. But remember, stay out of my study.'

'I don't even know how to get down to the basement, so how am I going to enter your precious room?' Marcus pointed out, resentment lending a hard edge to his words.

Nia gave him an assessing look. 'Seriously, Marcus, you gave me your word and I expect you to keep it.'

'I don't break my promises, Nia.'

Nia placed her hands on either side of his face. 'This may seem like a little thing to you. Insignificant even. But it's really important. Please don't even try to get down to the basement. Just leave it alone – okay? Otherwise you'll ruin things for both of us.'

Chapter Four ~ Marcus

THAT NIGHT AFTER NIA HAD DEPARTED on her gem-hunting expedition, Marcus lay in bed, but he couldn't sleep. He needed to stop interrogating his wife about her every movement and moment when she was away from him. Marcus knew he was upsetting Nia with the way he was acting, but he couldn't help himself. He didn't want to lose her but he knew that if he didn't fix his behaviour that would be exactly what happened. The past had taught him that if nothing else.

If you love her, then you have to trust her, he told himself.

But trust was a two-way street.

Why was Nia so insistent that he stay away from the basement? She never went down there until Marcus was safely installed in the attic. He'd particularly noticed that. And the house staircase started on the ground floor and provided access up to the attic but there were no stairs down to the basement – at least none that Marcus had ever seen. Was the basement entrance outside the house? Maybe there was a secret door in the summer house at the bottom of the garden. It was ridiculous that he didn't even know where the entrance was.

Why the big mystery?

What was she hiding down there?

Chapter Five ~ Nia

LIKE A VULTURE PROTECTING ITS FOOD, foreboding flapped its wings and dug its talons into Nia's chest. Practically every day Marcus asked to see her study and she always replied no but as the days had turned into weeks had turned into months, Marcus's manner of asking had changed, becoming less casual, more demanding.

Nia stared out of the plane window, looking down at the clouds drifting like ice floes beneath her. She tried to tell herself that she was worrying about nothing, but the sense of unease didn't leave her. In fact, with each passing minute, the feeling grew worse, not better. The vulture that had been occasionally pecking at her before was now ripping chunks out of her flesh.

Nia shook her head. No, Marcus wouldn't betray her, he just wouldn't. She wondered how many thousands of miles it would take before she started to believe that.

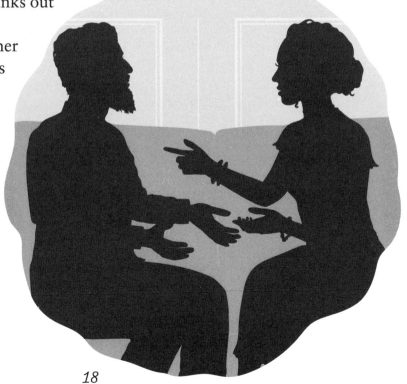

Chapter Six ~ Marcus

MARCUS WALKED ALL THE WAY around the house searching for a door or entrance that would lead down to the basement. Nia had been gone for six days and wasn't due back until the weekend, and though he missed her, he couldn't help begrudging Nia for not having faith in him. The idea of private spaces in their own home that he was not allowed to enter just didn't sit well with him.

Wives shouldn't have secrets from their husbands, he reasoned.

Every day, he walked around the perimeter of the house, he explored the garden, he searched the summer house and the garden shed but there were no inexplicable doors – not even the hint of one.

More determined than ever, he headed back into the house, examining each room for secret panels or disguised hidden entrances. A voice inside his head kept telling him to give it up, to stop what he was doing before it was too late – but he ignored it. He needed to see the basement – just once – then he'd never bother Nia about it again.

But having unsuccessfully examined the walls in every room for a hidden panel that would reveal a secret staircase which led down to the basement, Marcus finally reached the attic and had to admit defeat. Exhausted from his fruitless searches, he got into the lift and pressed the button for the ground floor. Feeling guilty, he took out his phone to text his wife.

He'd only just read Nia's reply when the phone slipped from his fingers, clattering to the floor. Squatting down to retrieve it, he

I miss you and can't wait for you to come home. Just thought I'd let you know. Marcus ♥

I miss you too. ♥ Looking forward to seeing you at the weekend. Don't do anything I wouldn't! Love you. Nia xx

glanced up before straightening and saw something he'd never seen before. The hard red button on the lift panel had a tiny lip on its underside, a small protrusion which it was impossible to see from above. Standing up, Marcus placed his index finger upon it and flicked it upwards revealing a silver lift button with a black B written upon it. Marcus didn't hesitate. He pressed it at once. The lift reached the ground floor, then continued downwards, descending slowly but surely into the bowels of the earth. Marcus estimated the lift went down at least two storeys before it juddered to a halt. He took a moment.

The air down here was overly warm and smelled strange. He could hear the whirr of distant machinery. An air-conditioning unit? The air had to be recycled this far down. Marcus pulled back the steel lattice door and stepped out of the lift. The floor was lined with grey slate tiles down a long corridor of unpainted brickwork. Halfway along the corridor was a plain wooden door but it was locked. At the end of the corridor were a set of oaken double doors crowded with carvings of vines and their fruit. Marcus reached out to stroke his fingers across a perfectly rendered bunch of grapes. Beads of sweat began to prick at his forehead and his armpits like jabbed warnings.

Don't do this. The voice inside his head was whispering on a loop.

Don't do this . . .

Marcus wanted his marriage to work – and it would once he had trained Nia in the proper way to behave. But he wasn't there yet. He'd seen the basement now, knew how to get to it. Point made, he should turn around.

But what lay beyond the doors?

Curiosity pulled him forward. His hands reached out for the handles. If these doors were locked too then Marcus already knew that he would dedicate his time before Nia returned home to hunting down the key. He turned the handles. The doors swung open.

Beyond lay Nia's domain.

Chapter Seven ~ Nia

GRIPPING HER SMARTPHONE, Nia watched through narrowed eyes as Marcus entered her study. Her heart was full to bursting. Over the previous few days via the hidden cameras installed throughout her home, she'd watched Marcus hunt high and low for the entrance to the basement. His explorations had made her cut her trip short.

And now the camera hidden behind the two-way mirror at the back of the lift had been activated as it always was whenever the basement button was pressed. Marcus hadn't hesitated in opening the doors to her study. He was about to do the one thing she had pleaded with him not to.

She'd really thought he might be the one.
She was wrong.
Now they were both going to pay for it.

Chapter Eight ~ Marcus

WAS THIS IT? SERIOUSLY?

Nia's huge basement study was lined on three sides with bookcases against the walls, each shelf filled to overflowing. In the middle of the room sat a behemoth of an ebony-wood desk with dual pedestals. On one side of the desk sat a laptop computer, a lamp, two huge wooden bowls filled with precious and semi-precious gems and some papers neatly stacked in a pile. On the other side of the desk were plastic containers filled with jewellery-making paraphernalia.

Marcus moved around the desk for a closer look at the papers but they were all related to buying gems and jewellery-making materials. Was there something in the desk perhaps? Something that explained all this concealment?

Each pedestal of the desk contained three drawers and a pen tray. Marcus examined the left-side pedestal first. More papers, pens, crystals and polished stones, bills. He could see no reason to hide any of those things away. Closing the drawers, he moved to the right of the desk. He opened the top drawer beneath the pen tray, only to jump back in revulsion, unable to believe his eyes. There, lined up in shallow glass containers, were a number of a particular body part – each resting on a bed of cotton wool.

'I'm deeply disappointed in you, Marcus,' Nia's voice sounded from the doorway.

Alarmed, Marcus shoved the drawer closed and stepped back, away from the horrifying spectacle, away from his wife whose hands were behind her back as if she were a dignitary inspecting an unsatisfactory specimen.

'What the hell, Nia?' Marcus pointed at the top drawer of her desk. 'What are all those doing in there? Please tell me they're plastic models.'

'I can't do that.'

'Why not?'

'Because they're real.'

Silence.

Marcus smiled uneasily. 'This is some kind of joke – right? Why would you keep those in a drawer?'

'Well, they have to be somewhere,' Nia shrugged. 'And each display case is hermetically sealed so they don't smell.'

'But why do you have them?'

'I collect them.'

Marcus stared, aghast. 'Why? From who?'

'From an ex-husband and others,' said Nia. 'Bullies like you who were too arrogant and full of themselves to listen. A police officer friend of mine told me all about you. You're so inadequate that you have to control your partner's every thought and action to feel better about yourself. It's quite pathetic. And the police have never been able to touch you because of your mum.'

'That's a lie,' Marcus denied furiously.

'Really? Speaking of lies, you implied you'd only been married once before. Not true. You've been married three times. Divorced twice from your first and third wives and your second wife died in a road accident before she could divorce you too. Those and all your other relationships have resulted in most of your partners having to involve the police because of your controlling, bullying, emotional and physical abuse. You're quite something, aren't you?'

'That was a long time ago. That's not me any more.'

'Then what're you doing down here when you gave me your word you'd leave my study alone?'

Marcus struggled to find an answer.

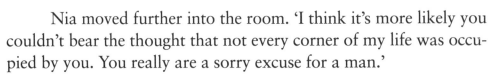

Nia moved further into the room. 'I think it's more likely you couldn't bear the thought that not every corner of my life was occupied by you. You really are a sorry excuse for a man.'

She took another step towards Marcus. He took a quick step back. That strange silky smile on her face was unnerving.

'Where are all the . . . others now?' asked Marcus.

Nia sighed. 'Who knows? Scattered up and down the country I presume. I leave it to my brother Jakob to sort out their final destination. They won't be bullying anyone else ever again, that's for sure.'

The temperature around Marcus dropped several degrees. Was she saying what he thought she was saying? Marcus shook his head. 'You weren't due back until the weekend.'

'I flew back yesterday. Something told me you wouldn't be able to resist trying to get down here. I've been here in my study ever since, and when you finally discovered how to get down here, I moved into the anteroom along the corridor to wait.'

The locked door Marcus had passed on the way to this room.

He glanced around. There, just below the ceiling, a tiny black sphere sat unobtrusively in the corner of the room. A camera – no doubt currently recording his smallest movement, his slightest expression.

'I had to know what you were hiding,' said Marcus.

'Oh, Marcus, this was a test – and you failed. Miserably. If you'd really changed, if you hadn't been so possessive, we could've lived together quite happily, even with all your secrets.'

Marcus cast an eye towards the closed drawer of Nia's desk, the one filled with body parts in glass cases. 'You can't talk to me about secrets.

You're ill, Nia. You need help. Let me get you the help you need.'

Nia sighed. 'Sooner or later, you all come down here, invading my privacy when I've specifically told you not to, and then you all say the same thing – that I'm the one who needs help. Well, not from where I'm standing.'

Marcus stared at Nia as if seeing her for the first time. She looked like his wife but there was a ruthlessness to her unrelenting gaze that Marcus had never seen before. Or maybe he had just never looked properly. His gaze dropped to the now closed drawer, the image he'd seen still looping inside his head. Marcus shivered. This room . . . this place . . . it was a trophy room with only one way in and out. Between him and the lift stood Nia. He had to get out of there. Get help. Phone the police. Nia was a stone-cold killer and he wasn't about to become her next victim.

Marcus drew himself up to his full height, his dark eyes blazing. 'Nia, you need to let me leave.'

'I can't do that.' Nia shook her head. 'I warned you what would happen if you came down here.'

Marcus wasn't prepared to listen to any more. He needed to get past Nia, and if that meant immobilising her by tying her up until the police arrived, then so be it.

Marcus hurtled around the huge desk and leapt towards her, full of resolve. Nia brought her right arm forward to reveal what she was holding. A taser. Marcus feinted to the right, then ducked to grab Nia's arm. They grappled for the weapon, toe-to-toe, chest-to-chest, barely a gap between their bodies. Marcus couldn't believe how strong she was. He had to get the taser away from her.

An elbow jab.

A kick.

He and Nia fell apart. A hiss as the taser fired.

A moment's silence.

Then a cry of agony echoed around the vast room. The discharged taser had found a target.

Chapter Nine - Nia

SHAKING HER HEAD, Nia stood over Marcus as he writhed on the floor. He was mere moments away from passing out completely. She watched him struggle to stay conscious, desperate to move his arms, his legs, any part of his body voluntarily. She walked away, only to return within moments holding a hypodermic syringe. Marcus's eyes followed her as she squatted down to place the needle against his throat. His body was still in shock, periodically twitching from the taser, so Nia knew he'd barely feel it when she injected the substance in the syringe into his body. His eyes began to flutter closed.

'Men like you need to learn that when a woman has a space of her own, you should keep out unless explicitly invited in. Why is that so hard to understand?'

Marcus opened his mouth but no sounds emerged.

'You should know the truth about me, Marcus. I do owe you that much. My great-great-great-great-great-grandfather was Aloysius Barbleue – more infamously known as just Bluebeard. After he was caught and killed, his children changed their names for their own protection and safety, and scattered across the world, but his story was passed down from generation to generation in my family. I am my ancestor's child.' Nia smiled without humour. 'It's ironic that I follow in his footsteps while trying to atone for what he did to so many women. So I want my real name to be the last thing you ever hear in this life. My name is Bluebeard, Nia Bluebeard.'

Marcus's eyes rolled back in his head and he knew no more.

Chapter Ten ~ One week later

NIA SAT AT THE DESK in her basement study, holding her favourite wedding photo of her and Marcus. She hadn't anticipated the wave of sadness that came over her as she looked at Marcus's smiling face. She really had liked him. Nia's first husband had been an abusive nasty piece of work. His death had been an accident. Self-defence. The demise of the ones who had followed him were not. Her best friend in the police service had provided the names and Nia had done the rest.

But in doing so, she realised she'd become the very thing she abhorred.

No more.

There would be no more husbands, no more partnerships. And when her time finally came, she would come down to this basement, disable the lift – and never leave. That would be her punishment and her penance. Nia opened the top desk drawer to her right. A single tear ran down her cheek. There, in a sealed, shallow glass case, sitting on top of all the other souvenirs and taking pride of place, sat Marcus's left ear.

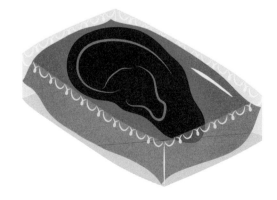

AFTERWORD

What I particularly love about fairy stories is that the fate of the protagonist tends to rest in their own hands. To paraphrase Heraclitus – the protagonist's character is their fate. The distinction between good and evil in fairy stories is always very clear, and though good doesn't always win, evil is, if not vanquished, then at least exposed for what it is. However, the fairy stories I grew up with were very different to the 'softer' variations that are currently told. When I was a child, they were much darker, far more brutal.

For example, in the very first 'Cinderella' story I read, the Prince was tricked into believing that each of Cinderella's stepsisters was his missing bride-to-be by them cutting off their toes or their heel to ensure their feet fitted into Cinderella's glass slipper. As he escorted each in turn back to his palace, the Prince had to have his attention drawn to the blood gushing out of the glass shoe before he knew he'd been duped. The first version of 'Little Red Riding Hood' I read had the poor child devoured by the Wolf when she pointed out what big teeth he had. The end. And though a number of these tales scared me, I devoured them. I read them over and over again until I could recite my favourite ones by heart.

'Bluebeard' was the first story I read which featured not just domestic violence but a serial killer – before I even knew either of those terms. Throughout my childhood, I read a number of versions of this story, each of which told the tale of a woman warned not to go into one specific locked room in her newly-wed husband's absence. I felt the story was grossly unfair! If Bluebeard really didn't want his wife to go into a locked room while he was away on business, then why give her the key? Was it merely a test to see if his wife was trustworthy? Or was he deliberately setting her up to fail? Did he really love her or was he simply seeking yet another victim?

In those stories I read, Bluebeard's behaviour was never questioned, that was just who and what he was. A given. The plight of his new wife, however, always got to me. What must it have been like to open the door to the locked room and be confronted by the bodies of all the other women Bluebeard had married and murdered? Truly horrific. In the original story, Bluebeard's wife is so terrified by what she sees that she drops the room key in the chamber of horrors, and it falls into a blood puddle. No matter how hard she tries, the blood can't be wiped or washed off because the key Bluebeard has given her is magic. The stain disappears from one side, only to appear on the other. Upon his return Bluebeard will have visual proof that his wife disobeyed his instructions. Even the inanimate objects are conspiring to bring about his wife's death. Yes, Bluebeard was killed with the help of his wife's brothers (I don't think I ever read a version where the wife was actually given a name), but the story was presented as a cautionary tale against women's curiosity. Victim-blaming.

So, is it any wonder that when I was invited to write my own version of a fairy story, 'Bluebeard' immediately sprang to mind? Not a watered-down version but the 'Bluebeard' of my childhood, retold. There was so much material to work with! As I considered the setting for my retelling – the past or the present – I weighed up the advantages and disadvantages each option would give me. I decided to go for a more modern-day retelling but with a viper's twist in the tale. In the present I wouldn't need magic keys, I could use technology instead to the same purpose. Don't get me wrong, I love magic! But I felt using it in this story without having it introduced as an everyday, ordinary occurrence would jar. I was also very interested in presenting a couple existing within a relationship which becomes increasingly more controlling and its consequences for all those involved.

The story I wanted to write had some questions to ask. In fighting back against that which we deplore, how do we stop ourselves from becoming deplorable? Was Heraclitus correct? Is a person's character truly their fate? Can the ends ever justify the means? I love stories which ask questions! I hope my version of 'Bluebeard' does exactly that.

2 4 6 8 10 9 7 5 3 1

Vintage
20 Vauxhall Bridge Road, London SW1V 2SA

Vintage Classics is part of the Penguin Random House group of companies
whose addresses can be found at global.penguinrandomhouse.com.

Penguin
Random House
UK

First published by Vintage Classics in 2020

www.vintage-books.co.uk

A CIP catalogue record for this book is available from the British Library

ISBN 9781784876418

Typeset and design by Friederike Huber

Printed and bound in China by C&C Offset Printing Co., LTD

Penguin Random House is committed to a sustainable future for our
business, our readers and our planet. This book is made from
Forest Stewardship Council® certified paper.